HIGH-SPEED TRAINS

Debbie Croft

Contents

Fast Trains

Throughout the world, there are many trains that travel from one city to another at very high speeds. Most of these trains only carry passengers, although some transport goods, too.

The E6 Series *Shinkansen* is a very fast train that operates in the Akita Prefecture in Japan.

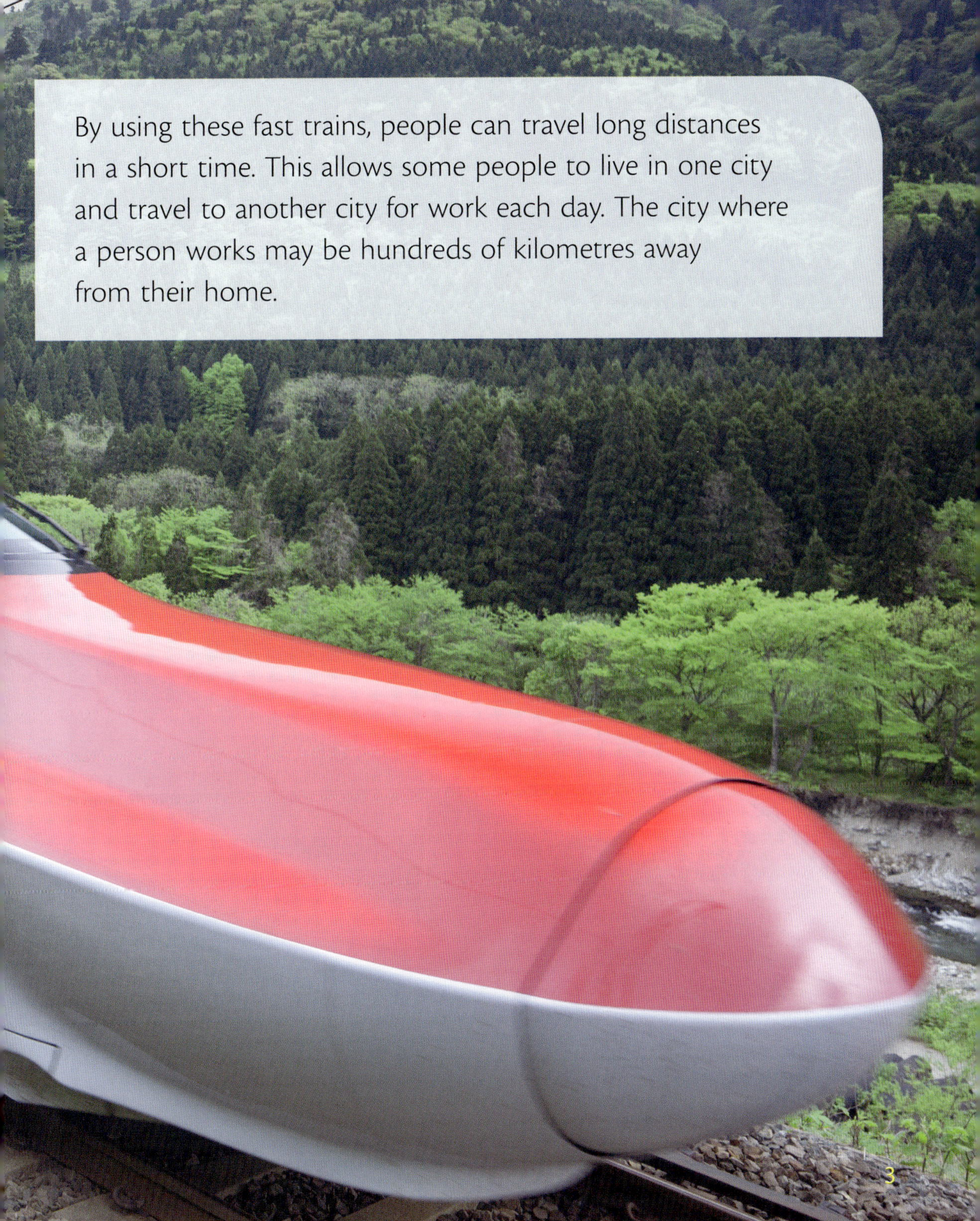

By using these fast trains, people can travel long distances in a short time. This allows some people to live in one city and travel to another city for work each day. The city where a person works may be hundreds of kilometres away from their home.

Although most trains travel quickly, only certain trains can be called "fast trains". These trains must have each of the following three special features:

1. Fast trains must travel on tracks that have been specially built for high-speed travel. Sometimes, an existing track can be used, but it has to be improved so it is suitable and safe for trains that can travel much faster. Most of the time, a special track is built for the new trains.

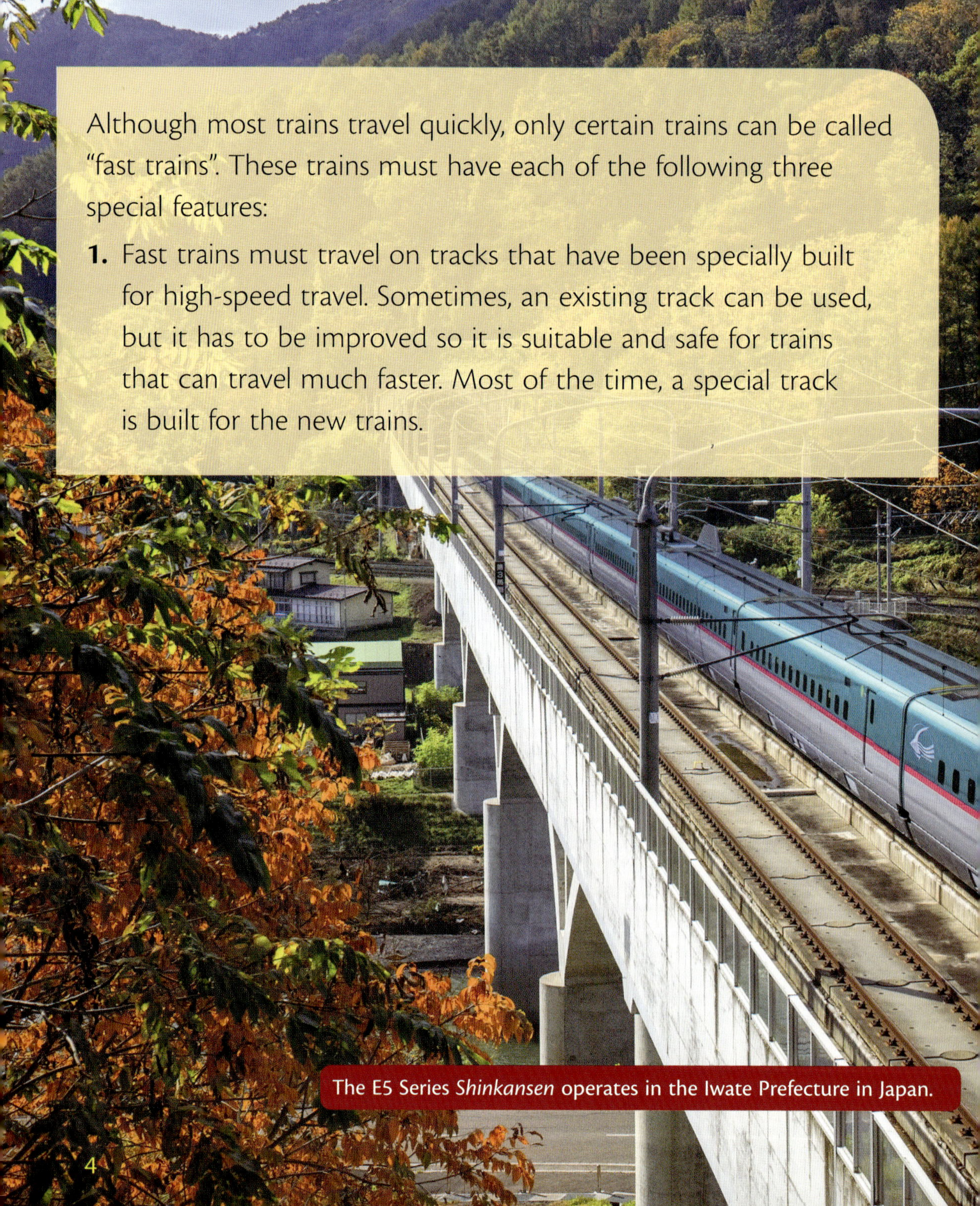

The E5 Series *Shinkansen* operates in the Iwate Prefecture in Japan.

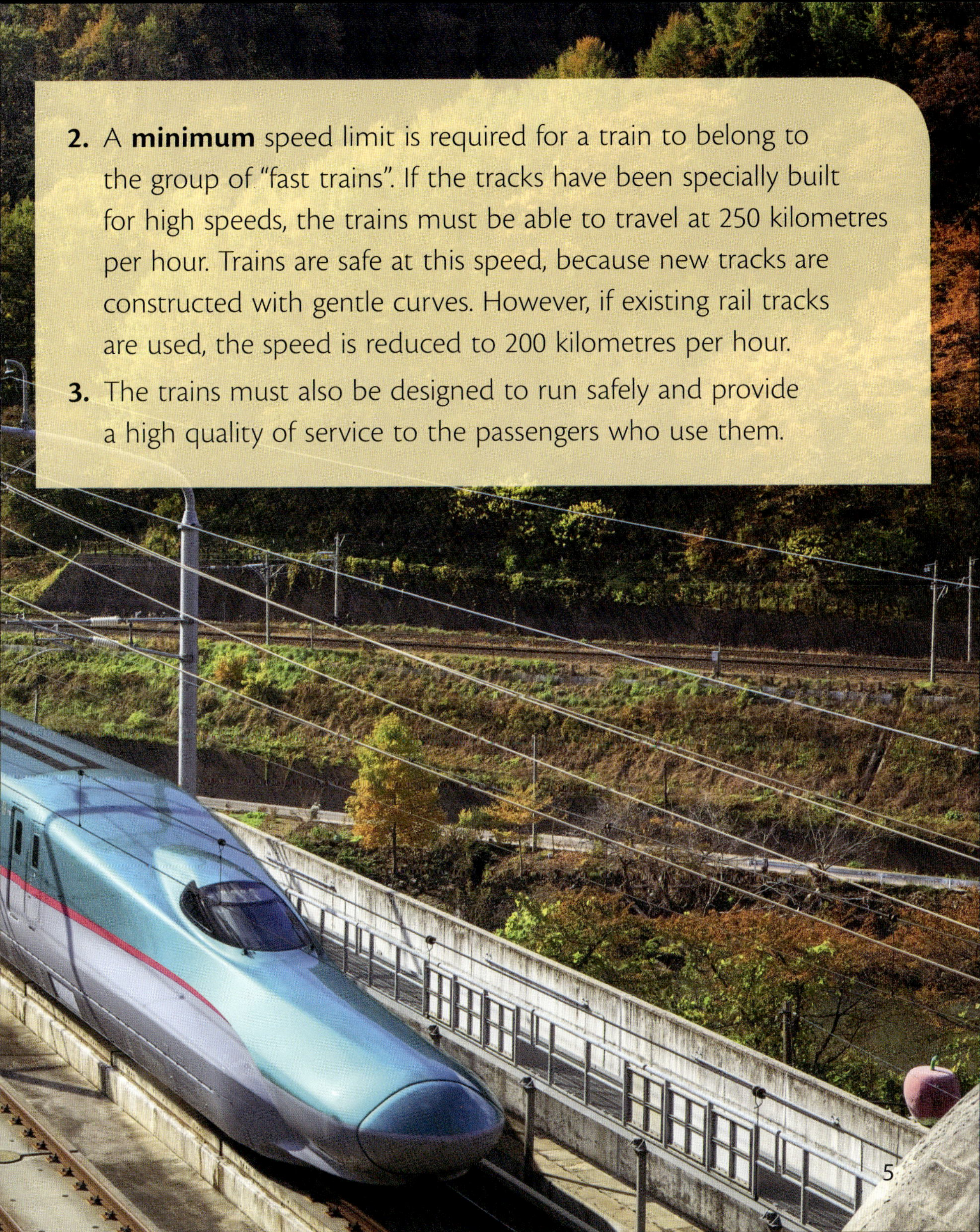

2. A **minimum** speed limit is required for a train to belong to the group of "fast trains". If the tracks have been specially built for high speeds, the trains must be able to travel at 250 kilometres per hour. Trains are safe at this speed, because new tracks are constructed with gentle curves. However, if existing rail tracks are used, the speed is reduced to 200 kilometres per hour.
3. The trains must also be designed to run safely and provide a high quality of service to the passengers who use them.

Fast Trains Around the World

Today, Japan, China, South Korea, Taiwan, Germany, Spain, Italy, France, Belgium and the United Kingdom all have trains that belong to the special group of vehicles known as "fast trains".

Locations of Fast Trains Around the World

The *Shinkansen*

Japan was the first country to build railway lines **specifically** for high-speed travel. Japan's first fast train line was called the *Shinkansen*. The trains on this line were nicknamed "bullet trains", because they could reach very high speeds. Unlike older trains, these trains were **tapered** at the front, to allow air to flow smoothly over the top and around the train. The bullet trains were developed in time to carry passengers from **outlying** areas into Tokyo for the 1964 Olympic Games.

The *Eurostar*

The *Eurostar* is a high-speed rail service that connects London, in the United Kingdom, with Paris, in France, and Brussels, in Belgium. The trains on the *Eurostar* **network** travel through a very long tunnel under the English Channel. This tunnel links the United Kingdom with Europe. The *Eurostar* service has the longest underwater section anywhere in the world. It is also the second longest rail tunnel in the world.

A *Eurostar* train exits the Channel tunnel in France.

This train is popular because it is fast and easy to use. Trains on this line travel at up to 300 kilometres per hour. Passengers travelling on the *Eurostar* can avoid waiting in long **queues**; they can board the train much quicker than passengers can board a plane at an airport. This high-speed rail network can move passengers from the centre of London to the centre of Paris faster than passengers who travel by plane.

The *Talgo 350*

The Spanish *Talgo 350* trains are unusual because they have wheels set in pairs that are not joined by **axles**. The pairs of wheels are located between the railcars, rather than underneath each car. This design feature allows the train to travel at higher speeds, even on curves. It also reduces swaying movements and lowers the noise level, so passengers enjoy a smoother, quieter ride.

These trains travel between Madrid and Barcelona, and Madrid and Valladolid, at speeds of up to 330 kilometres per hour.

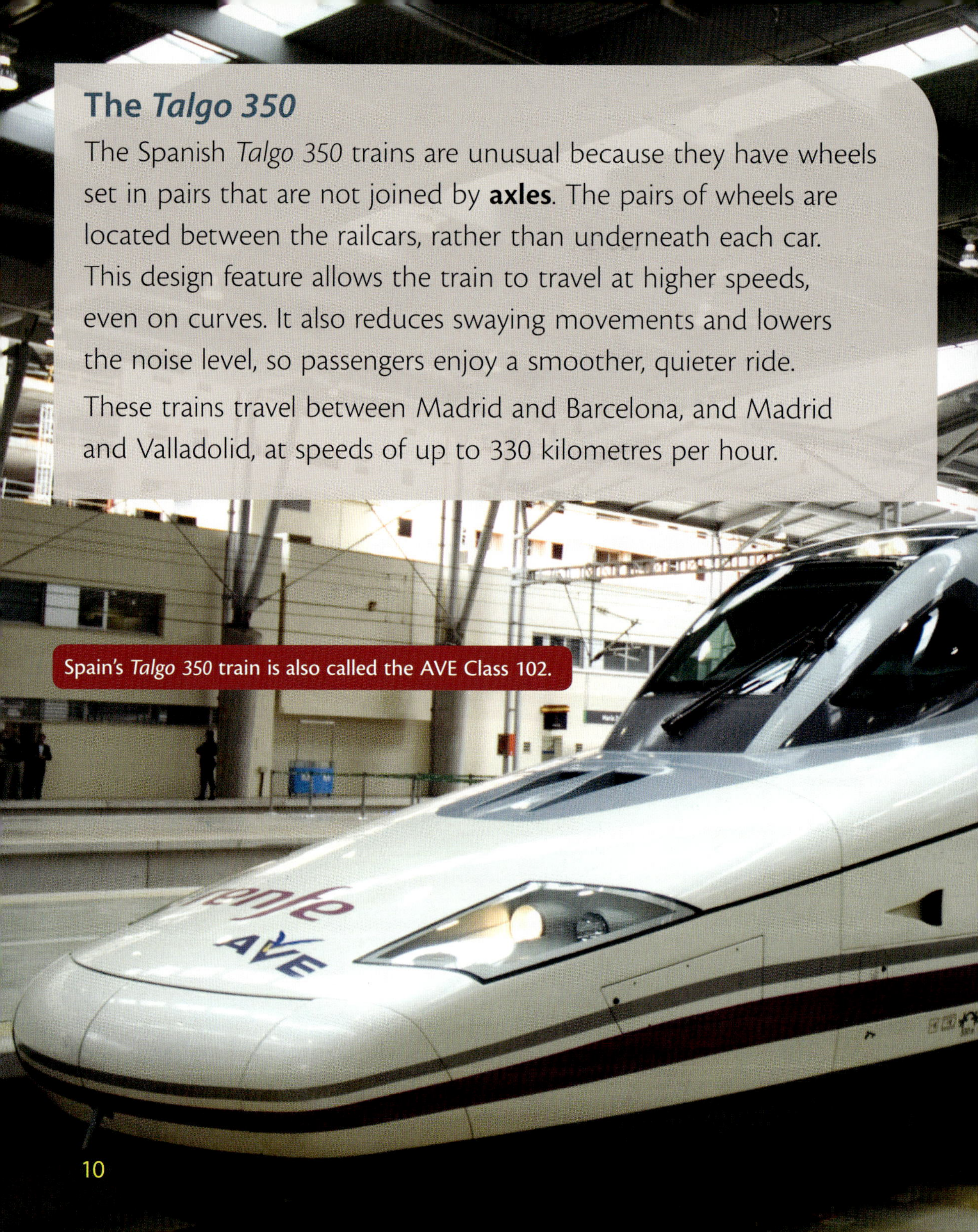

Spain's *Talgo 350* train is also called the AVE Class 102.

Think and Talk About ...

The *Talgo 350* is nicknamed "*Pato*", which means "duck" in Spanish.

The *Harmony CRH380A*

Until recently, the fastest train in the world was in China. This train is called the *Harmony CRH380A*. It can reach a maximum speed of 486 kilometres per hour, though it only travels at 350 kilometres per hour when it is carrying passengers.

The development of this train began early in 2008. In October 2010, it began a regular service. When the *Harmony CRH380A* was introduced, the travel time from Shanghai to Hangzhou was reduced from 1 hour and 18 minutes to just 45 minutes.

The train is well known for its good-quality ride at a very high speed. It is well **insulated**, so it provides a quiet journey for the passengers. The cars are made from aluminium, which is a lightweight metal. Lighter trains are able to travel faster because there is less mass to move along the track.

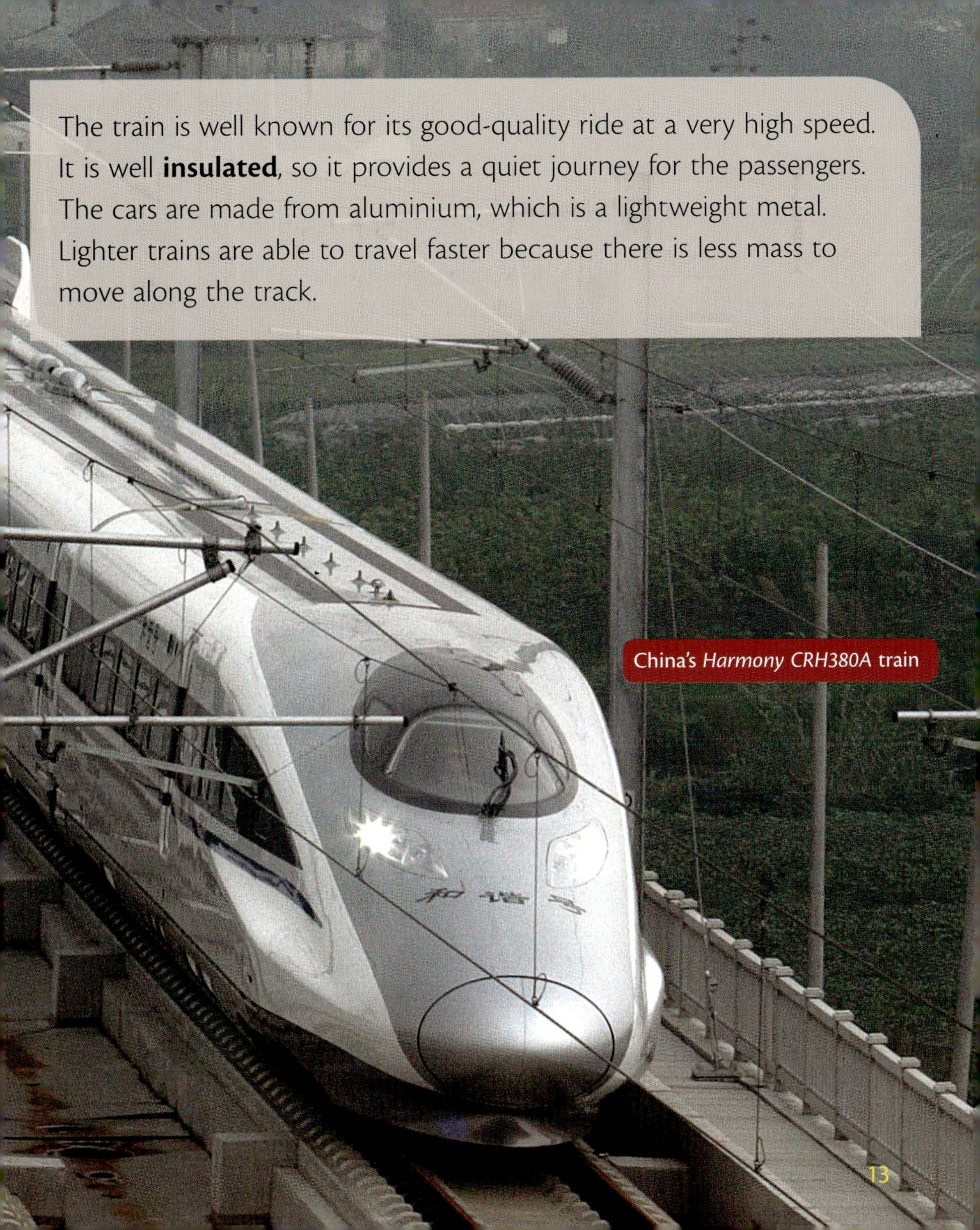

China's *Harmony CRH380A* train

Maglev Trains

The fastest trains in the world are called "maglev" trains. Maglev is a shortened form of the words "magnetic levitation". Unlike other trains, maglev trains have no wheels. Instead, they run along a guide rail. Magnets underneath the train push the cars away from the magnets in the guide rail. The trains appear to levitate, or float on air.

Maglev trains don't have an engine like most other trains, so they do not use fossil fuels to create power. Instead, the train is pulled along by more magnets in the guide rail. Scientists believe maglev trains are a better choice, because they cause less damage to the environment.

These modern trains also have a **streamlined** body, so they can travel at higher speeds. The design for the front of each train is smooth and **sleek**, similar to the fast trains that run on rail tracks.

Shanghai's maglev train

Think and Talk About ...

Maglev systems greatly reduce the amount of time and money spent on repairs to tracks and railcars.

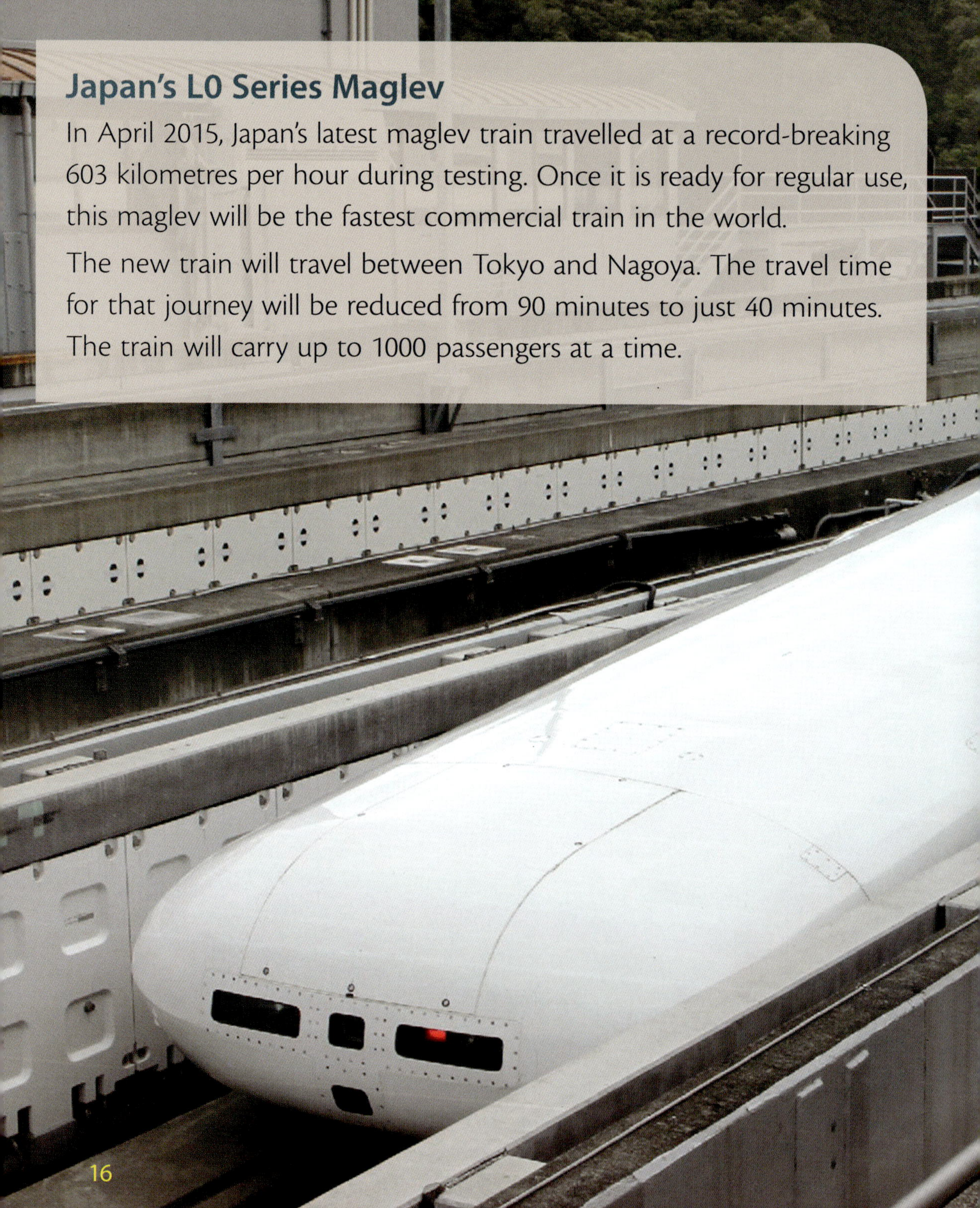

Japan's L0 Series Maglev

In April 2015, Japan's latest maglev train travelled at a record-breaking 603 kilometres per hour during testing. Once it is ready for regular use, this maglev will be the fastest commercial train in the world.

The new train will travel between Tokyo and Nagoya. The travel time for that journey will be reduced from 90 minutes to just 40 minutes. The train will carry up to 1000 passengers at a time.

Japan's record-breaking L0 series maglev train

Think and Talk About ...

It is nearly impossible for a maglev train to derail.

Although modern trains around the world travel at very high speeds, they also have excellent safety records. In some areas where fast trains operate, many people choose to travel on trains instead of planes.

Trains are quicker and easier to board and are therefore becoming more popular than air travel.

Think and Talk About ...

Even though some trains can travel much faster, trains are usually only allowed to reach a maximum speed of 320 kilometres per hour.

Today, there are many different kinds of *Shinkansen* trains.

How the First Fast Train Was Developed

In 1964, Japan's bullet train was introduced as part of the *Shinkansen* rail network. This was the first transport **system** designed to allow trains to travel at very high speeds. For many years, Japan's bullet train held the record for being the fastest train in the world.

Special technology was developed to create trains that could travel safely at speeds much greater than regular passenger trains. There were four main improvements put in place to ensure the safety and comfort of rail passengers travelling at high speeds.

The first *Shinkansen* train was launched in time for the Tokyo Olympic Games in 1964.

1. Designing the First Bullet Train

The design of the *Shinkansen* trains was a very important factor in how fast they could travel. To reach a speed of 200 kilometres per hour, trains needed to be **aerodynamic**. This meant that the front of the train had to be tapered and as smooth as possible. This shape allowed the air to flow up over the top of the train, rather than pushing against the front and slowing it down.

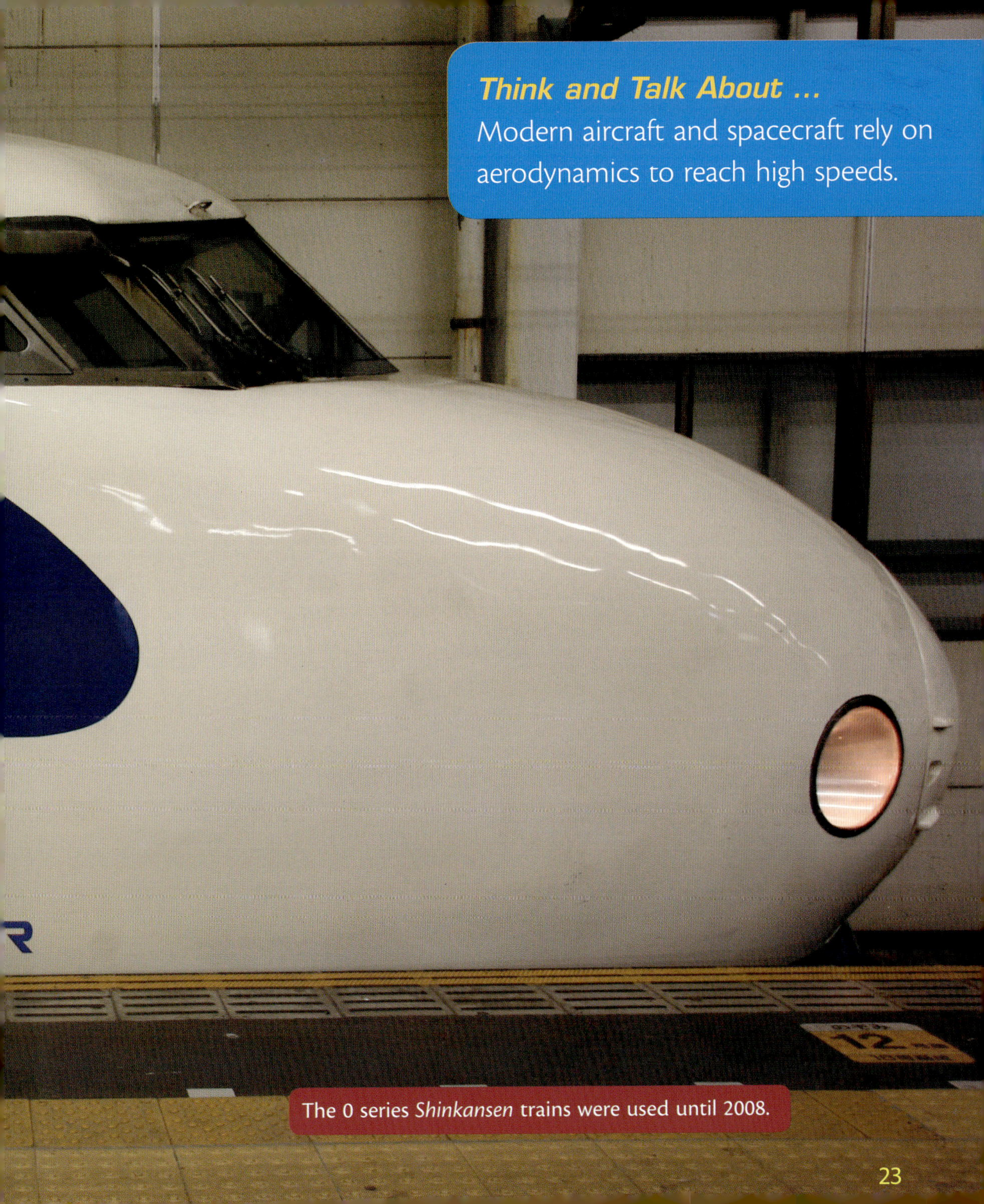

Think and Talk About ...

Modern aircraft and spacecraft rely on aerodynamics to reach high speeds.

The 0 series *Shinkansen* trains were used until 2008.

The gentle curves of the new rail tracks meant the *Shinkansen* didn't have to slow down for corners.

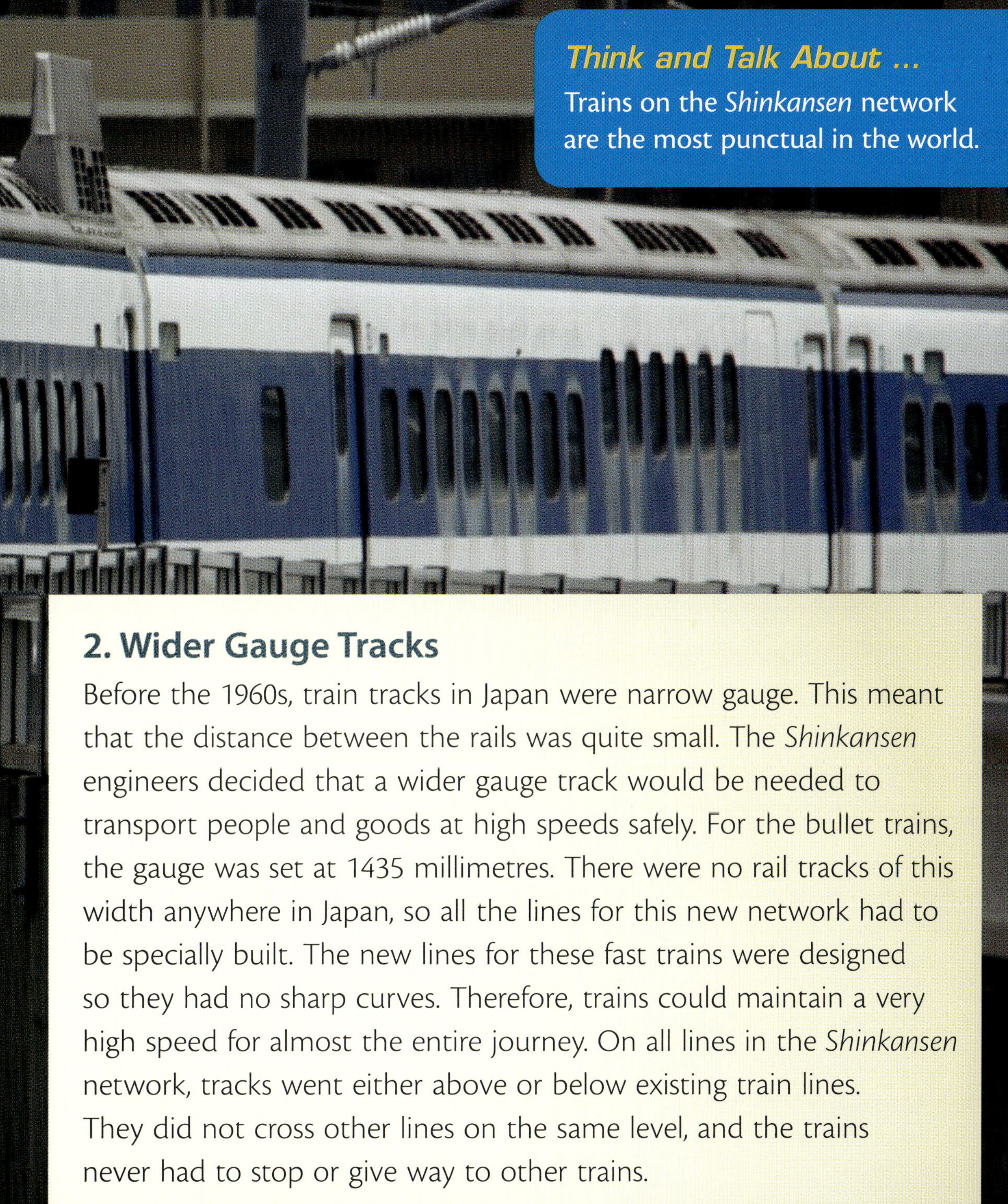

Think and Talk About ...

Trains on the *Shinkansen* network are the most punctual in the world.

2. Wider Gauge Tracks

Before the 1960s, train tracks in Japan were narrow gauge. This meant that the distance between the rails was quite small. The *Shinkansen* engineers decided that a wider gauge track would be needed to transport people and goods at high speeds safely. For the bullet trains, the gauge was set at 1435 millimetres. There were no rail tracks of this width anywhere in Japan, so all the lines for this new network had to be specially built. The new lines for these fast trains were designed so they had no sharp curves. Therefore, trains could maintain a very high speed for almost the entire journey. On all lines in the *Shinkansen* network, tracks went either above or below existing train lines. They did not cross other lines on the same level, and the trains never had to stop or give way to other trains.

3. Reducing Vibration

In the 1960s, all trains had wheels and ran on rails. When these trains reached high speeds, the wheels **vibrated** on the tracks. This vibration caused some of the passenger cars to vibrate, too. After travelling long distances, if the vibration was strong enough, the passenger cars became damaged.

the interior of a 0 series *Shinkansen* train

To prevent this damage, the bottom of the bullet trains' passenger cars were fitted with air springs. These springs greatly reduced the vibration from the wheels. Small vibrations did not reach the passenger cars, and the people on board enjoyed a smoother, more comfortable ride.

4. Automatic Train Control

On most trains, the driver changes the train's speed by following signals that are placed along the track. However, it would have been almost impossible for the driver of a bullet train to read signals, because the train travelled at such a high speed. This meant a new speed-control system had to be developed. This system became known as ATC, or Automatic Train Control. Information about safe travelling speeds was sent along the track, to be received by a signal attached to the driver's seat. Then, the train automatically **adjusted** to the correct speed.

A driver sits at the controls of a 500 series *Shinkansen* train.

A special traffic-control system also made sure that there was enough time and distance between the trains running on the same line. This meant the trains always remained a safe distance apart.

Since the introduction of the *Shinkansen* bullet trains, many other countries have developed high-speed rail systems. The bullet train no longer holds the record for the world's fastest train. However, it was the use of these four basic technologies that allowed Japan to lead the way in the development of fast-train networks.

fast trains lined up at a station in Tokyo, Japan

Glossary

adjusted *(verb)*	changed slightly
aerodynamic (*adjective*)	shaped so that air flows smoothly over the top
axles *(noun)*	the bars that connect and turn the wheels of a vehicle
insulated *(verb)*	protected from temperature or noise
minimum *(adjective)*	the least amount
network *(noun)*	an arrangement of different parts
outlying *(adjective)*	distant; away from the centre of the city
queues *(noun)*	long lines of people waiting to be served
sleek *(adjective)*	smooth, elegant
specifically *(adverb)*	for a particular purpose
streamlined *(adjective)*	smoothly shaped
system *(noun)*	a way of doing things
tapered *(verb)*	smoothly narrowing or thinning
vibrated *(verb)*	shook or shuddered

Index